Best Friends

Om KIDZ
An imprint of Om Books International

First Published in 2023

Om Kidz | Om Books International

Corporate & Editorial Office
A-12, Sector 64, Noida 201 301
Uttar Pradesh, India
Phone: +91 120 477 4100
Email: editorial@ombooks.com
Website: www.ombooksinternational.com

Sales Office
107, Ansari Road, Darya Ganj
New Delhi 110 002, India
Phone: +91 11 4000 9000
Email: sales@ombooks.com

ISBN: 978-93-94547-19-3

Printed in India

10 9 8 7 6 5 4 3 2 1

Best Friends

I'm all set to read

Paste your photograph here

My name is

May had a little **brother** Joey. She loved to **play with** him.

May was also **very** fond of Lily, her best **friend**.

One day, Lily's **father said**, 'I **have** bought train **tickets** for us to go and **visit** May.'

Lily jumped with excitement.

In the afternoon, May got a call **from** Lily.

"I am coming to **visit** you!" she **said**. May was **very** happy!

"**This** is great news,"
shouted May.
"I cannot **wait** to see you,"
said Lily.

May was **very** happy.

She told Joey **that** Lily was **coming**,

Joey was happy too.

He started **clapping with** joy.

Joey **watched** a cartoon on T.V. before **going** to bed.

His Mom had allowed him to **watch** a cartoon for half an hour before bedtime.

May fell **asleep**.
She dreamt of all
the exciting things
she and Lily **would** do.

Lily was excited too. She could not **sleep** the whole **night**. She **could** not wait to be **with** her best **friend**.

When the **doorbell** rang the next day, May ran to the **door**.

Lily had **arrived**.
She was **holding**
a **bouquet**.

Her dad had **dropped** her at May's **house**. He had gone **away** to meet a **friend**.

The frolic had begun. The two **friends hugged**!

Joey **clapped**.
They were all going
to **have** a great time
together.

May and Lily **went** to **watch** a movi

Their dads sat behind **them**.

They ate **popcorn** and **nachos**.

Mom and Joey stayed at **home**.

May, Lily and Joey
went to the fair.
They had a lot of fun.

Lily **went** home the next day.
She promised to come **again**.

Know Your Words

Sight Words

again
away
could
from
have
said
that
them
this
very
went
when
with
would

Naming Words

bouquet
brother
door
doorbell
father
friend
home
house
nachos
night
popcorn
tickets

Doing Words

arrived
asleep
clapped
clapping
coming
crying
dropped
going
holding
hugged
play
shouted
sleep
visit
wait
watch